IT was Old Bear's birthday, and the toys were getting ready for a party in the garden. Little Bear and his friend Elsie were busy wrapping presents.

'Look what I've got for Old Bear!' said Elsie.

Little Bear looked at the funny-shaped present.

'Is it a walking stick?' he asked.

'NOT a walking stick,' laughed Elsie. 'It's an umbrella. Look, I painted it myself!'

'Old Bear will love that,' said Bramwell Brown. 'Are you going to wrap it?'

'I'll just tie a bow round it,' said Elsie, 'I'm good at bows!'

ELSIE began to tie ribbons on all the parcels, but they looked so nice she just couldn't stop.

'Slow down, Elsie,' gasped Little Bear, 'I haven't finished *one* bow yet!'

'And you're meant to be tying up *presents*,' grumbled Duck, 'not tying up *me!*'

'WOULD anyone like to help me with the balloons?'
asked Jolly Tall.
'Yes please!' said Elsie, 'I'm good at blowing up balloons!'
Little Bear chose small balloons, while Elsie blew up long,
curly ones and twisted them into funny shapes with her trunk.

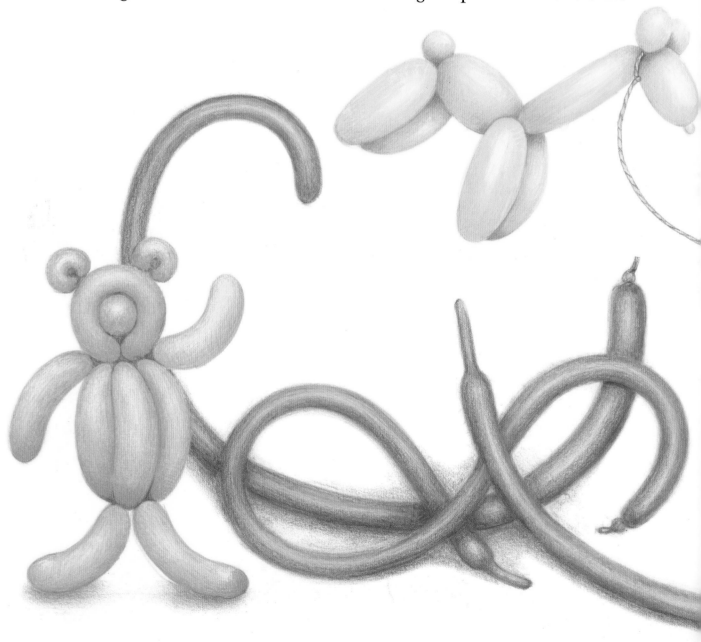

'LOOK, this one's for Old Bear,' she cried.

'That's amazing,' said Little Bear, 'an anteater!'

'It's an elephant,' laughed Elsie, 'not an anteater.'

'Old Bear *will* be surprised,' said Jolly. 'I bet he's never seen a balloon elephant before.'

Just then Bramwell Brown called from the kitchen, 'Who would like to decorate Old Bear's cake?'

'ME, me!' cried Elsie, 'I'm good at cakes!' She began to cut up pieces of fruit. 'Oh dear!' she said, 'I've dropped some on the floor. Look out!'

But Bramwell didn't hear; he slipped on a blueberry and landed, bump, right on top of the cake.

'Oh no,' groaned Little Bear. 'Half the cake's flat. We can't eat it now.'

'The other half's alright,' said Elsie. 'We can cut it down the middle and put the squashed bit underneath!'

T HEY had nearly finished decorating the half-a-cake
when Sailor marched in banging a tambourine.

'Would you like to join our band?' he asked. 'We're going to
play "Happy Birthday" for Old Bear.'

'That sounds fun,' said Little Bear, 'I'll play my drum.'

'CAN I play too?' asked Elsie. 'I'm good at music!'
She stood on tiptoe, stretched out her trunk, and blew:

'WHEEEEEEEEEEEEEEEEE'

'I'm not sure that's Old Bear's sort of music,' said Duck.
'Come on,' said Little Bear, 'let's take the
cake outside.'

IN the garden, Little Bear and Elsie found the
bubble mixture and began to blow big,
wibbly-wobbly bubbles.
'Old Bear loves bubbles,' said Elsie.
'He does,' muttered Duck, 'but not
all over his cake.'

'I KNOW what we need,'
said Elsie. She hurried indoors and
returned with the birthday umbrella.
'Old Bear won't mind if we borrow it,' she said, holding
it over the cake. 'Look! The bubbles can't land now.'

  'So all we need is Old Bear,' said Bramwell, 'and the party
can begin.'

  'Here I am!' called a familiar voice. 'Goodness, you have
been working hard.'

BUT just as Old Bear arrived, a gust of wind caught the umbrella and lifted Elsie right up in the air.

'Help!' she called. 'Get me down! I'm *not* good at *flying*!'

Little Bear tried to catch her feet but the wind blew her higher and higher.

'What do we do now?' he cried.

HOOT, the owl, heard the noise from her nest on top of the wardrobe and quickly flew into the garden to see what was happening.

'Oh Hoot,' gasped Little Bear, 'Elsie's blown away! Now we can't even see her.'

'Don't worry,' said Hoot kindly, 'I'm sure I can find her.'
With a flap of her wings, she took off and disappeared
over the trees.

'Poor Elsie,' said Old Bear. 'I do hope she's alright!'

THE toys stared anxiously at the sky. All they could see were clouds.

Suddenly Hoot reappeared carrying something in her beak.

'She's got the umbrella,' cried Little Bear, 'but where's Elsie?'

Then they saw: sitting inside the umbrella and holding on tight was a very excited little elephant!

'HOORAY!' they cheered as Hoot landed on the grass. 'Well done Hoot; you found her!'

'Hello everyone,' laughed Elsie as she jumped out of the umbrella and lifted it up above her head. 'Old Bear, this is actually your birthday present. I didn't mean to fly away with it!'

'THANK YOU Elsie,' said Old Bear. 'It's lovely. But getting you back safely is the best present I could have wished for. What an exciting birthday!'

And while Old Bear was undoing the bows on his parcels, his friends made a few little changes to his cake.

'It's an umbrella cake,' whispered Elsie.

'HAPPY BIRTHDAY OLD BEAR!'

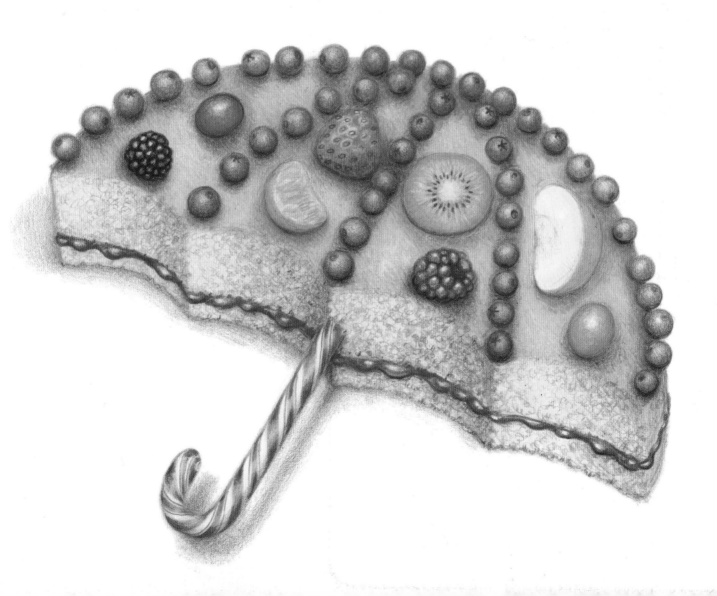

For Wren

SALARIYA
SCRIBO BOOK HOUSE SCRIBBLERS

This edition published in Great Britain in MMXXI by Scribblers,
an imprint of The Salariya Book Company Ltd
25 Marlborough Place,
Brighton BN1 1UB

www.salariya.com
www.janehissey.co.uk

HB ISBN-13: 978-1-910706-72-5
PB ISBN-13: 978-1-913337-64-3

1 3 5 7 9 8 6 4 2

A CIP catalogue record for this book is available from the British Library.

Printed and bound in China.
Printed on paper from sustainable sources.